Grimm, Beauty and the Beast by Jeanne-Marie Leprince de Beaumont and Rapunzel as told by Jacob Grimm and Wilhelm Grimm THE MONSTER The Legend of Sleepy Hollow by Washington Irving, Frankenstein by M

Newbery and Brahms' Lullaby by Johannes Brahms THE MOON Around the Moon by Jules Verne THE WORLD The Wonderful Wizard of Oz by L. Frank Baum, The Wind in the Willows by Kenneth Grahame, L

ark Twain, A Christmas Carol by Charles Dickens, Moby Dick by Herman Melville, The Secret Garden by Frances Hodgson Burnett, Heidi by Johanna Spyri, Black Beauty and His K

Count of Monte Cristo by Alexandre Dumas, Kidnapped by Robert Louis Stevenson, Gulliver's Travels by Jonathan Swift and Twenty Thousand Leagues Under the Sea vels by Jon

Wonderland by Lewis Carroll THE MOUNTAINS Peter Pan and Wendy by J.M. Barrie THE CAVE Treasure Island by Robert Louis Stevenson and Kidnapped Little Re

mm and Wilhelm Grimm, Snow White and Rose Red as told by Jacob Grimm and Wilhelm Grimm, Beauty and the Beast by Jeanne-Marie Leprince de Beaumont and Rapu m THE

yan, Twinkle, Twinkle, Little Star by Jane Taylor, Hush-a-Bye Baby as adapted by John Newbery and Brahms' Lullaby by Johannes Brahms THE MOON Around t he Wonder

rroll, Great Expectations by Charles Dickens, Adventures of Huckleberry Finn by Mark Twain, A Christmas Carol by Charles Dickens, Moby Dick by Herman Melville, The Secret Garden t, Heidi by

wiss Family Robinson by Johann David Wyss, Robinson Crusoe by Daniel Defoe, The Count of Monte Cristo by Alexandre Dumas, Kidnapped by Robert Louis Stevenson, Gulliver's Travels by Jonathan Swift and Twenty Thousa

nd Leagues Under the Sea by Jules Verne THE HOLE Alice's Adventures in Wonderland by Lewis Carroll THE MOUNTAINS Peter Pan and Wendy by J.M. Barrie THE CAVE Treasure Island by Robert Lou

Grimm, Tom Thumb as told by Richard Johnson, The Golden Bird as told by Jacob Grimm and Wilhelm Grimm, Snow White and Rose Red as told by Jacob Grimm and Wilhelm Grimm, Beauty and the Beast by Jeanne-Marie Lep

Grimm and Wilhelm Grimm THE CLOUDS Suo Gân as adapted by Robert Bryan, Twinkle, Twinkle, Little Star by Jane Taylor, Hush-a-Bye Baby as adapted by John Newbery and Brahms' Lullaby by Johannes Brahms T

Tale of Peter Rabbit by Beatrix Potter, Alice's Adventures in Wonderland by Lewis Carroll, Great Expectations by Charles Dickens, Adventures of Huckleberry Finn by Mark Twain, A Christmas Carol by Charles Dickens, Mob

Irving THE SEA The Voyages of Doctor Dolittle by Hugh Lofting, The Swiss Family Robinson by Johann David Wyss, Robinson Crusoe by Daniel Defoe, The Count of Monte Cristo by Alexandre Dumas, Kidnapped b

David Wyss, The Adventures of Pinocchio by Carlo Collodi and Twenty Thousand Leagues Under the Sea by Jules Verne THE HOLE Alice's Adventures in Wonderland by Lewis Carroll THE MOUNTAINS Peter P

d Wilhelm Grimm, The Golden Goose as told by Jacob Grimm and Wilhelm Grimm, Tom Thumb as told by Richard Johnson, The Golden Bird as told by Jacob Grimm and Wilhelm Grimm, Snow White and Rose Red as told by J

helley and Dracula by Bram Stoker THE ROPE Rapunzel as told by Jacob Grimm and Wilhelm Grimm THE CLOUDS Suo Gân as adapted by Robert Bryan, Twinkle, Twinkle, Little Star by Jane Taylor, Hush-a-Bye B

men by Louisa May Alcott, The Three Musketeers by Alexandre Dumas, The Tale of Peter Rabbit by Beatrix Potter, Alice's Adventures in Wonderland by Lewis Carroll, Great Expectations by Charles Dickens, Adventures of Hu

Sir Thomas Malory and Sir James Knowles and Rip Van Winkle by Washington Irving THE SEA The Voyages of Doctor Dolittle by Hugh Lofting, The Swiss Family Robinson by Johann David Wyss, Robinson Crusoe by D

obinson Crusoe by Daniel Defoe, The Swiss Family Robinson by Johann David Wyss, The Adventures of Pinocchio by Carlo Collodi and Twenty Thousand Leagues Under the Sea by Jules Verne THE HOLE Alice's Adve

d by Jacob Grimm and Wilhelm Grimm, Hansel & Gretel as told by Jacob Grimm and Wilhelm Grimm, The Golden Goose as told by Jacob Grimm and Wilhelm Grimm, Tom Thumb as told by Richard Johnson, The Golden Bird a

ER The Legend of Sleepy Hollow by Washington Irving, Frankenstein by Mary Shelley and Dracula by Bram Stoker THE ROPE Rapunzel as told by Jacob Grimm and Wilhelm Grimm THE CLOUDS Suo Gân as

of Oz by L. Frank Baum, The Wind in the Willows by Kenneth Grahame, Little Women by Louisa May Alcott, The Three Musketeers by Alexandre Dumas, The Tale of Peter Rabbit by Beatrix Potter, Alice's Adventures in Won

yri, Black Beauty by Anna Sewell, The Legends of King Arthur and His Knights by Sir Thomas Malory and Sir James Knowles and Rip Van Winkle by Washington Irving THE SEA The Voyages of Doctor Dolittle by Hu

s Under the Sea by Jules Verne THE WAVE Gulliver's Travels by Jonathan Swift, Robinson Crusoe by Daniel Defoe, The Swiss Family Robinson by Johann David Wyss, The Adventures of Pinocchio by Carlo Collodi and

Kidnapped by Robert Louis Stevenson THE FOREST Little Red Cap as told by Jacob Grimm and Wilhelm Grimm, Hansel & Gretel as told by Jacob Grimm and Wilhelm Grimm, The Golden Goose as told by Jacob Grimm an

d Rapunzel as told by Jacob Grimm and Wilhelm Grimm THE MONSTER The Legend of Sleepy Hollow by Washington Irving, Frankenstein by Mary Shelley and Dracula by Bram Stoker THE ROPE Rapunzel as to

nd the Moon by Jules Verne THE WORLD The Wonderful Wizard of Oz by L. Frank Baum, The Wind in the Willows by Kenneth Grahame, Little Women by Louisa May Alcott, The Three Musketeers by Alexandre Dum

Melville, The Secret Garden by Frances Hodgson Burnett, Heidi by Johanna Spyri, Black Beauty by Anna Sewell, The Legends of King Arthur and His Knights by Sir Thomas Malory and Sir James Knowles and Rip Van Winkle b

son, Gulliver's Travels by Jonathan Swift and Twenty Thousand Leagues Under the Sea by Jules Verne THE WAVE Gulliver's Travels by Jonathan Swift, Robinson Crusoe by Daniel Defoe, The Swiss Family Robinson by

arrie THE CAVE Treasure Island by Robert Louis Stevenson and Kidnapped by Robert Louis Stevenson THE FOREST Little Red Cap as told by Jacob Grimm and Wilhelm Grimm, Hansel & Gretel as told by Jacob Gr

Grimm, Beauty and the Beast by Jeanne-Marie Leprince de Beaumont and Rapunzel as told by Jacob Grimm and Wilhelm Grimm THE MONSTER The Legend of Sleepy Hollow by Washington Irving, Frankenstein by M

Newbery and Brahms' Lullaby by Johannes Brahms THE MOON Around the Moon by Jules Verne THE WORLD The Wonderful Wizard of Oz by L. Frank Baum, The Wind in the Willows by Kenneth Grahame, L

ark Twain, A Christmas Carol by Charles Dickens, Moby Dick by Herman Melville, The Secret Garden by Frances Hodgson Burnett, Heidi by Johanna Spyri, Black Beauty by Anna Sewell, The Legends of King Arthur and His K

Count of Monte Cristo by Alexandre Dumas, Kidnapped by Robert Louis Stevenson, Gulliver's Travels by Jonathan Swift and Twenty Thousand Leagues Under the Sea by Jules Verne THE WAVE Gulliver's Travels by Jon

Wonderland by Lewis Carroll THE MOUNTAINS Peter Pan and Wendy by J.M. Barrie THE CAVE Treasure Island by Robert Louis Stevenson and Kidnapped by Robert Louis Stevenson THE FOREST Little Re

mm and Wilhelm Grimm, Snow White and Rose Red as told by Jacob Grimm and Wilhelm Grimm, Beauty and the Beast by Jeanne-Marie Leprince de Beaumont and Rapunzel as told by Jacob Grimm and Wilhelm Grimm THE

yan, Twinkle, Twinkle, Little Star by Jane Taylor, Hush-a-Bye Baby as adapted by John Newbery and Brahms' Lullaby by Johannes Brahms THE MOON Around the Moon by Jules Verne THE WORLD The Wonde

rroll, Great Expectations by Charles Dickens, Adventures of Huckleberry Finn by Mark Twain, A Christmas Carol by Charles Dickens, Moby Dick by Herman Melville, The Secret Garden by Frances Hodgson Burnett, Heidi by

wiss Family Robinson by Johann David Wyss, Robinson Crusoe by Daniel Defoe, The Count of Monte Cristo by Alexandre Dumas, Kidnapped by Robert Louis Stevenson, Gulliver's Travels by Jonathan Swift and Twenty Thousa

nd Leagues Under the Sea by Jules Verne THE HOLE Alice's Adventures in Wonderland by Lewis Carroll THE MOUNTAINS Peter Pan and Wendy by J.M. Barrie THE CAVE Treasure Island by Robert Lou

Grimm, Tom Thumb as told by Richard Johnson, The Golden Bird as told by Jacob Grimm and Wilhelm Grimm, Snow White and Rose Red as told by Jacob Grimm and Wilhelm Grimm, Beauty and the Beast by Jeanne-Marie Lep

Grimm and Wilhelm Grimm THE CLOUDS Suo Gân as adapted by Robert Bryan, Twinkle, Twinkle, Little Star by Jane Taylor, Hush-a-Bye Baby as adapted by John Newbery and Brahms' Lullaby by Johannes Brahms T

Tale of Peter Rabbit by Beatrix Potter, Alice's Adventures in Wonderland by Lewis Carroll, Great Expectations by Charles Dickens, Adventures of Huckleberry Finn by Mark Twain, A Christmas Carol by Charles Dickens, Mob

Irving THE SEA The Voyages of Doctor Dolittle by Hugh Lofting, The Swiss Family Robinson by Johann David Wyss, Robinson Crusoe by Daniel Defoe, The Count of Monte Cristo by Alexandre Dumas, Kidnapped b

David Wyss, The Adventures of Pinocchio by Carlo Collodi and Twenty Thousand Leagues Under the Sea by Jules Verne THE HOLE Alice's Adventures in Wonderland by Lewis Carroll THE MOUNTAINS Peter P

d Wilhelm Grimm, The Golden Goose as told by Jacob Grimm and Wilhelm Grimm, Tom Thumb as told by Richard Johnson, The Golden Bird as told by Jacob Grimm and Wilhelm Grimm, Snow White and Rose Red as told by J

helley and Dracula by Bram Stoker THE ROPE Rapunzel as told by Jacob Grimm and Wilhelm Grimm THE CLOUDS Suo Gân as adapted by Robert Bryan, Twinkle, Twinkle, Little Star by Jane Taylor, Hush-a-Bye B

men by Louisa May Alcott, The Three Musketeers by Alexandre Dumas, The Tale of Peter Rabbit by Beatrix Potter, Alice's Adventures in Wonderland by Lewis Carroll, Great Expectations by Charles Dickens, Adventures of Hu

Sir Thomas Malory and Sir James Knowles and Rip Van Winkle by Washington Irving THE SEA The Voyages of Doctor Dolittle by Hugh Lofting, The Swiss Family Robinson by Johann David Wyss, Robinson Crusoe by D

obinson Crusoe by Daniel Defoe, The Swiss Family Robinson by Johann David Wyss, The Adventures of Pinocchio by Carlo Collodi and Twenty Thousand Leagues Under the Sea by Jules Verne THE HOLE Alice's Adve

d by Jacob Grimm and Wilhelm Grimm, Hansel & Gretel as told by Jacob Grimm and Wilhelm Grimm, The Golden Goose as told by Jacob Grimm and Wilhelm Grimm, Tom Thumb as told by Richard Johnson, The Golden Bird a

ER The Legend of Sleepy Hollow by Washington Irving, Frankenstein by Mary Shelley and Dracula by Bram Stoker THE ROPE Rapunzel as told by Jacob Grimm and Wilhelm Grimm THE CLOUDS Suo Gân as

of Oz by L. Frank Baum, The Wind in the Willows by Kenneth Grahame, Little Women by Louisa May Alcott, The Three Musketeers by Alexandre Dumas, The Tale of Peter Rabbit by Beatrix Potter, Alice's Adventures in Won

yri, Black Beauty by Anna Sewell, The Legends of King Arthur and His Knights by Sir Thomas Malory and Sir James Knowles and Rip Van Winkle by Washington Irving THE SEA The Voyages of Doctor Dolittle by Hu

s Under the Sea by Jules Verne THE WAVE Gulliver's Travels by Jonathan Swift, Robinson Crusoe by Daniel Defoe, The Swiss Family Robinson by Johann David Wyss, The Adventures of Pinocchio by Carlo Collodi and

Kidnapped by Robert Louis Stevenson THE FOREST Little Red Cap as told by Jacob Grimm and Wilhelm Grimm, Hansel & Gretel as told by Jacob Grimm and Wilhelm Grimm, The Golden Goose as told by Jacob Grimm an

d Rapunzel as told by Jacob Grimm and Wilhelm Grimm THE MONSTER nkenstein by Mary Shelley and Dracula by Bram Stoker THE ROPE Rapunzel as to

nd the Moon by Jules Verne THE WORLD The Wonderful Wizard of Oz Grahame, Little Women by Louisa May Alcott, The Three Musketeers by Alexandre Dum

Melville, The Secret Garden by Frances Hodgson Burnett, Heidi by Johanna Spyri, hur and His Knights by Sir Thomas Malory and Sir James Knowles and Rip Van Winkle b

son, Gulliver's Travels by Jonathan Swift and Twenty Thousand Leagues Under ls by Jonathan Swift, Robinson Crusoe by Daniel Defoe, The Swiss Family Robinson by

arrie THE CAVE Treasure Island by Robert Louis Stevenson and Kidnapped by Robert Louis Stevenson THE FOREST Little Red Cap as told by Jacob Grimm and Wilhelm Grimm, Hansel & Gretel as told by Jacob Gr

First published 2016 by Walker Books Ltd
87 Vauxhall Walk, London SE11 5HJ

2 4 6 8 10 9 7 5 3 1

Extract from "The Speed of Darkness" taken from Muriel Rukeyser's *The Speed of Darkness,* New York:
Random House, 1968, included here with kind permission of ICM Partners™, New York

This book was hand-lettered and the typographical landscapes
were typeset in Adobe Garamond Pro.

Printed in China

MIX
Paper from
responsible sources
FSC® C008047

British Library Cataloguing in Publication Data:
a catalogue record for this book is available from the British Library

ISBN 978-1-4063-5831-5

www.walker.co.uk

WALKER BOOKS
AND SUBSIDIARIES
LONDON • BOSTON • SYDNEY • AUCKLAND

A Child of Books

Oliver JEFFERS
SAm winston

For Lila, from Sam
For Luella, from Oliver

"The universe is made of stories, not of atoms."
Muriel Rukeyser, "The Speed of Darkness", 1968

And for Hurbinek

"Hurbinek died in the first days of March 1945, free but not redeemed.
Nothing remains of him: he bears witness through these words of mine."
Primo Levi, *If This Is a Man / The Truce*, 1947

I am a
child of BOOKS.

I come from
a WORLD of STORIES

Once upon a time
there was a child who
loved to read

and upon my
IMAGINATION

The Voyages of Doctor Dolittle It was all so new and different: just the sky above ship, which was to be our house and our street, our home and our garden, for so many days t so tiny in all this wide water – so tiny and yet so snug, sufficient, safe. I looked around me an a deep breath. The Doctor was at the wheel steering the boat which was now leaping and plu through the waves. (I had expected to feel seasick at first but was delighted to find that I didn't.) had been told off to go downstairs and prepare dinner for us. Chee-Chee was coiling up ropes in the rn and laying them in neat piles. My work was fastening down the things on the deck so that nothing roll about if the weather should grow rough when we got further from the land. Jip was up in the peak boat with ears cocked and nose stuck out – like a statue, so still – his keen old eyes keeping a sharp look-r floating wrecks, sand-bars, and other dangers. Each one of us had some special job to do, part of the pro nning of a ship. Even old Polynesia was taking the sea's temperature with the Doctor's bath-thermome ed on the end of a string, to make sure there were no icebergs near us. As I listened to her swearing to herself because she couldn't read the pesky figures in the fading light, I realized that the voyage gun in earnest and that very soon it would be night – my first night at sea! *Robinson Crusoe* Ao rowed, or rather driven about a league and a half, as we reckoned it, a raging wave, mountai , came rolling astern of us, and plainly bade us expect the coup de grace. It took us with such that it overset the boat at once; and separating us as well from the boat as from one another, g not time to say, "O God!" for we were all swallowed up in a moment. Nothing can describe th fusion of thought which I felt, when I sunk into the water; for though I swam very well, yet I c not deliver myself from the waves so as to draw breath, till that wave having driven me, or ra arried me, a vast way towards the shore, and having spent itself, went back, and left me upon n and almost dry, but half dead with the water I took in. I had such presence of mind, as well as ft, that seeing myself nearer the mainland than I expected, I got upon my feet, and endeavour make on towards the land as fast as I could before another wave should return and take me up ; but I soon found it was impossible to avoid it; for I saw the sea come after me as high as a gr l, and as furious as an enemy, which I had no means or strength to contend with: my business htful shock, which threw everyone to the deck, and seemed to threaten her immediate uction. Dreadful sounds betokened the breaking up of the ship, and the roaring water hold my breath, and raise myself upon the water if I could; and so, by swimming, to preserve , and pilot myself towards the shore, if possible, my greatest concern now being that the s uld carry me a great way towards the shore when it came on, might not carry me back again t when it gave back towards the sea. *The Swiss Family Robinson* Amid the roar of the thu es I suddenly heard the cry of "Land! land!", while at the same instant the ship struck wi ed in on all sides. Then the voice of the captain was heard above the tumult, shoutin wer away the boats! We are lost!" "Lost!" I exclaimed, and the word went like a dag my heart; but seeing my children's terror renewed, I composed myself, calling out fully, "Take courage, my boys! We are all above water yet. There is the land not far, et us do our best to reach it. You know God helps those that help themselves!" W at, I left them and went on deck. What was my horror when through the foam a ray I beheld the only remaining boat leave the ship, the last of the seamen sprin her and push off, regardless of my cries and entreaties that we might be allowed d even had the crew wished it, the return of the boat was impossible. Casting peless, inasmuch as the stern of the ship containing our cabin was jammed be two high rocks, and was partly raised from among the breakers which dashed orepart to pieces. As the clouds of mist and rain drove past, I could make out, gh rents in the vaporous curtain, a line of rocky coast, and, rugged as it was, p will never sail more, she is so placed that our cabin will remain above water, omorrow, if the wind and waves abate, I see no reason why we should not get a *The Count of Monte Cristo* He saw overhead a black and tempestuous sky, ac the wind was driving clouds that occasionally suffered a twinkling star to appe fore him was the vast expanse of waters, sombre and terrible, whose waves foame roared as if before the approach of a storm. Behind him, blacker than the sea, bla han the sky, rose phantom-like the vast stone structure, whose projecting crags see ike arms extended to seize their prey, and on the highest rock was a torch lighting t gures. He fancied that these two forms were looking at the sea: doubtless these stran diggers had heard his cry. Dantès dived again, and remained a long time beneath th This was an easy feat to him, for he usually attracted a crowd of spectators in the bay the lighthouse at Marseilles when he swam there, and was unanimously declared to be t st swimmer in the port. When he came up again the light had disappeared. "Sometimes," n my voyages, when I was a man and commanded other men, I have seen the heavens

I Float.

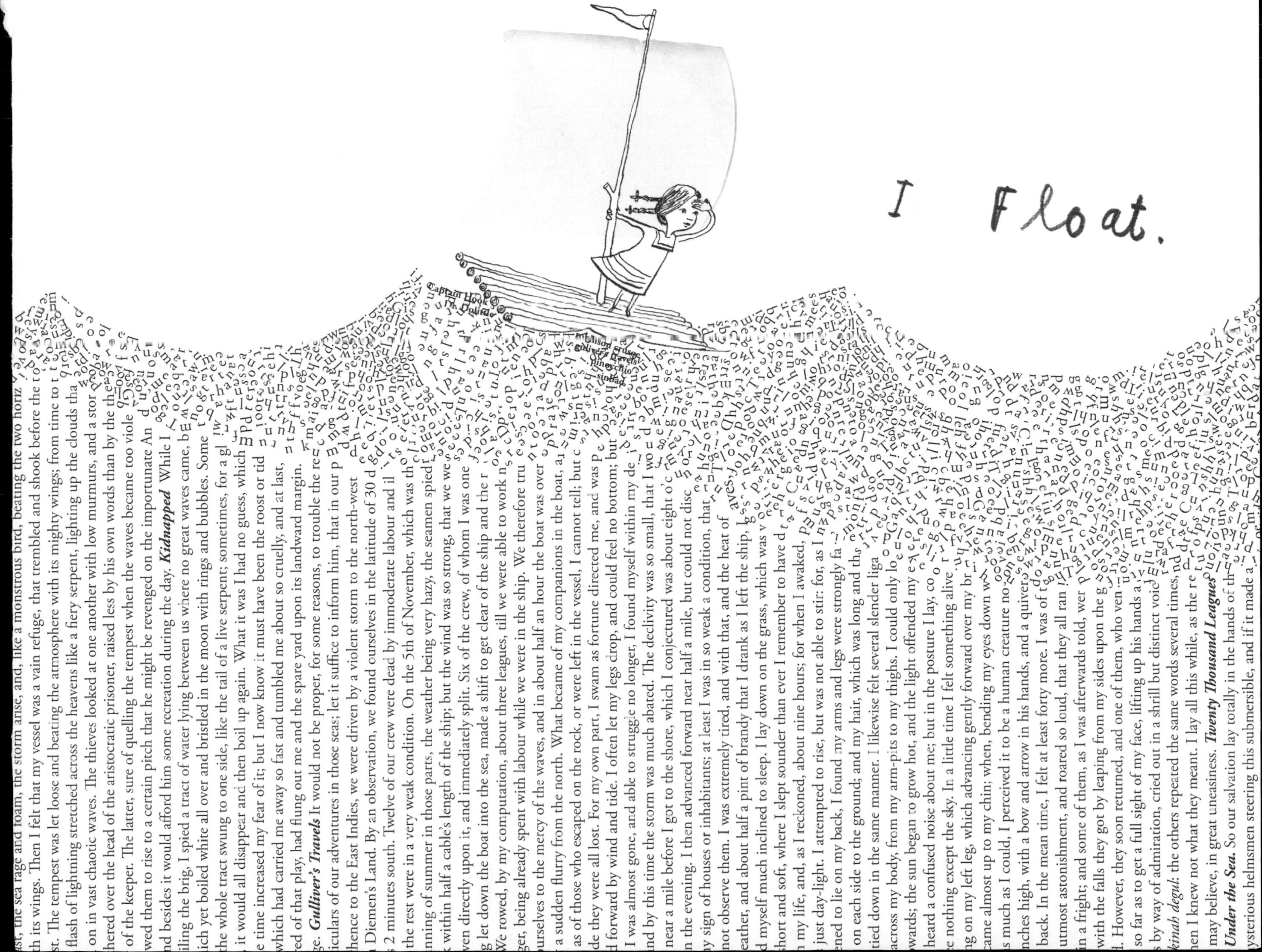

of in south... summer which was i those parts, beginning to being very hazy, the seamen spied a rock within It not be proper, for some reasons, n the seamen spied a rock within It but the wind was so strong, that half a cable's length of the ship; were driven directly upon it, and **Gulliver's Travels** Six of t were driven directly upon it, and e crew, of whom I was one, having le t down the boat into the sea, made a s hift to get clear of the ship and the rock. e rowed, by my computation, about three es, till we were able to work no longer, bei g already spent with labour while we were i ng already spent with labour while we were i the ship. We therefore trusted ourselves to the une directed me, and in about half an hour the boat of the waves, and in about half an hour the boat overset by a sudden flurry from the north. What be of my companions in the boat, as well as of those who caped on the rock, or were left in the vessel, I cannot tell; b ut conclude they were all lost. For my own part, I swam as f une directed me, pushed forward by wind and tide. I often let my legs drop, and felt no bottom; but when I was almost gone, able to struggle no longer, I found myself within my depth; and me the storm was much abated. Six times had the darkness closed over a wild an we had been tempest-tossed. Six times had the darkness closed over a wild an d terrific scene, and returning light as often brought but renewed distress, for the raging storm increased in fury until on the seventh day all hope was lost. conjecture could be formed as to our whereabouts. The crew had lost heart, and were utterly exhausted by incessant labour. The riven masts had gone by the board, leaks had been sprung every direction, and the water, which rushed in, gained upon us rapidly. Instead of reckless oaths, the seamen now uttered frantic cries to God for mercy, mingled with strange and often us vows, to be performed should deliverance be granted. Every man on board alternately commended his soul to his Creator, and strove to bethink himself of some means of savin ful peril: if not, let us calmly yield our lives into His hand, and think of the joy and blessedness of finding ourselves for ever and ever united in that happy home above." I ds my weeping wife looked bravely up, and, as the boys clustered round her, she began to cheer and encourage them with calm and loving words. I rejoiced to see r was ready to break as I gazed on my dear ones. We knelt down together, one after another praying with deep earnestness and emotion. Fritz, in particular, h d deliverance for his dear parents and brothers, as though quite forgetting himself. Our hearts were soothed by the never-failing comfort of child-like our situation seemed less overwhelming. "Ah," thought I, "the Lord will hear our prayer! He will help us." **The Adventures of Pinocchio** "Wh asked Pinocchio of a little old woman. The water is very rough, and we're afraid he will be drowned." "Where is the little boat?" "There. Straight d of him across the ocean. The water is very rough, and we're afraid he will be drowned." "Where is the little boat?" "There. Straight d ered the little old woman, pointing to a tiny shadow, no bigger than a nutshell, floating on the sea. Pinocchio looked closely f es. And Pinocchio, standing on a high rock, tired out with searching, waved to him with hand and cap and even looked as if Geppetto, though far away from the shore, recognized his son; for he took off his cap and waved it also. Just then a huge wave came and the boat disappeared. They waited and waited for it, but it was g derstand that he would come back if he were able, but the sea was so heavy that he could do nothing to m was heard. Turning around, the fisher folk on the shore, whispering a prayer as they turned to go home. Just then 'll save him! I'll save my father!" The Marionette, being made of wood, float and swam like a fish in the rough water. Now and again he disappeared r once more. In a twinkling; he was far away from land. At last h ly lost to view. "Poor boy!" cried the fisher folk on the shore, and then gave a sharp cry: "It's my father!" Meanwhile, the little boat, tossed about by the angry waters, appeared and di d Leagues Under the Sea Near four o'clock in mumbled a few prayers, as they returned home. submersible picked up speed. We could f said the fisher folk on the shore this dizzying rush, and the waves se rose range. Fortunately Ned topside of this and we

I have SAILED
across a SEA
of WORDS

To ask if you will
come AWAY with me.

SOME PEOPLE have
FORGOTTEN where
I live

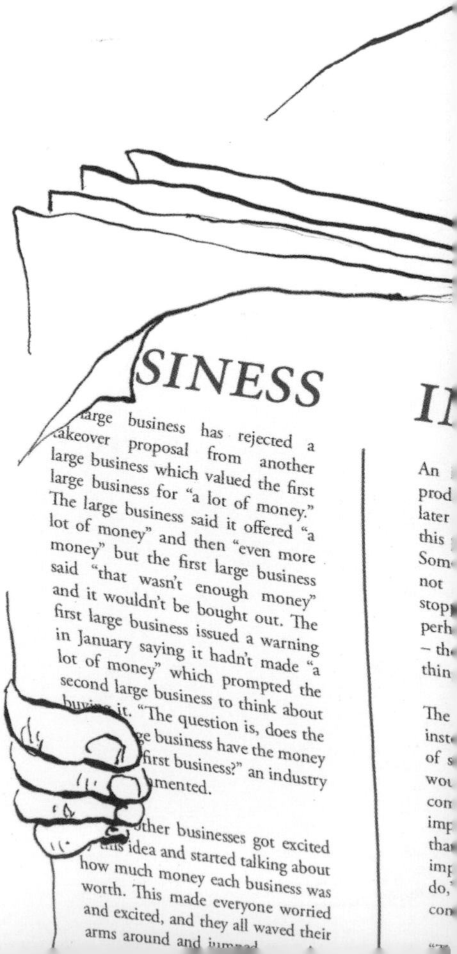

SINESS

I

large business has rejected a
takeover proposal from another
large business which valued the first
large business for "a lot of money."
The large business said it offered "a
lot of money" and then "even more
money" but the first large business
said "that wasn't enough money"
and it wouldn't be bought out. The
first large business issued a warning
in January saying it hadn't made "a
lot of money" which prompted the
second large business to think about
buying it. "The question is, does the
large business have the money
first business?" an industry
commented.

other businesses got excited
this idea and started talking about
how much money each business was
worth. This made everyone worried
and excited, and they all waved their
arms around and jumped

An
prod
later
this
Som
not
stop
perh
– the
thin

The
inste
of s
wou
com
imp
that
imp
do,
con

IMPORTANT THINGS

...rtant company is to stop
...g some important stuff by
...year. It said no one wanted
...cular bit of important stuff.
... from a website said – "It's
... surprising that they have
... producing this thing –
...'s not so important after all
...n issue now is to find other
...at might be important."

...pany announced it would
...ocus on producing other bits
...that they hoped the public
...nd important. "We remain
...ed to providing people with
...t things and if we can't do
...n we will pretend they are
...t and hopefully that will
...the leading inventor at the

also said they would stop making this
particular bit of stuff as they also thought
it might not be as important as they once
thought it was. "What makes something
really important nowadays is how much
money we spend on it and if we spend
vast amounts of money on it, then that
obviously means it's going to be really
important and we will certainly make a
hoo-haa about it when we put it in the
shops," said the Big Boss.

One customer did respond to this
comment with "My cat is very important
and that didn't cost anything!" to which
the important company wrote a letter
in response that said, "Dear Customer,
we understand that you think your cat
is very important but unfortunately you
are wrong in this matter. Our leading
inventor says he didn't im...

Serious Stuff

A group of serious people passed on concerns about a serious document that has been lost by a serious
organization. The serious people asked officials a long time ago to "look carefully" at this
document – the serious organization initially said it had looked at this serious document last ye...
concluded that "it wasn't that serious" and then went on to say "we have lost it." Someone els...
looked at this document said "actually it was serious and I hope they find it." In an earlier vers...
story, we reported that the serious
organization had started looking
for the serious document. In fact,
they started looking last year.
So far they have looked "under
chairs, rugs, and even down a
sofa." Someone suggested to try
looking "on the computer," but
that was unsuccessful as it wasn't
turned on.

In other cases like this – when
someone says "this is serious" and
the other says "no it isn't" – they
often have to find a third person
to tell them whether it's serious
One of the problems with
...e people

THE FACTS

Scientists have discovered a
new fact. In one test, nearly
half the subjects proved the
fact, it was revealed. The
findings, which came from
first watching people and
then quizzing them, have
attracted criticism from some
other scientists.

The paper, published in a
magazine about facts, said
that their fact was true.
A professor, who led the
research at a university, said:
"Our study demonstrated
...t it might

kind of thing but for th...
who don't – it could be rather
alarming.

In fact, other researchers in
the field have said the findings
are overstated. The authors
say this 'fact' might have
been overlooked in research.
Their work began with several
trials involving people who
were shut in a small room
and tested. After 6, 12, or 15
minutes, they were asked if
they had discovered this fact.
On average, their answers
were near the middle of a
...e point scale.

"It
is
a long
tail, certainly,"
said Alice,
looking down
with wonder at
the Mouse's tail;
"but why do you
call it sad?" And
she kept puzzling
about it while the
Mouse was speaking,
so that her idea of the
tale was something like
this: "Fury said to a mouse,
That he met in the house, 'Let
us both go to law: I will prosecute
YOU.—Come, I'll take no
denial; We must have a trial:
For really this morning I've
nothing to do.' Said the mouse
to the cur, 'Such a trial, dear sir,
With no jury or judge, would
be wasting our breath.' 'I'll be
judge, I'll be jury,' said cunning
old Fury: 'I'll try the whole cause, and
condemn you to death.' *Alice's Adventures
in Wonderland* The rabbit-hole went strai
then dipped suddenly down, so sud   that Alice had not a
moment to think about sto   lf before she found herself falling down what seemed to be a very deep well.
Either the well was very deep, or she fell very slowly, for she had plenty of time as she went down to look about her, and to

nothing of tumbling down stairs! How brave they'll all think me at home! W

Down, down, down. Would the fall never come to an

getting somewhere near the centre

Presently she began

But along these WORDS
I can show you the WAY.

wonder what was going to happen next. First, she tried to look down and make out what but it was too dark

y, I wouldn't say anything about it, even if I fell off the top of the was very likely true

end? "I wonder how many miles I've fallen by this time aloud. "I must

of the earth. Let me see: that would be four thousand miles down,

gain. "I wonder if I shall fall right through the earth How funny

Down, down, down. There was nothing else to do so Alice soo

WE will TRAVEL over
MOUNTAINS of MAKE-BELIEVE

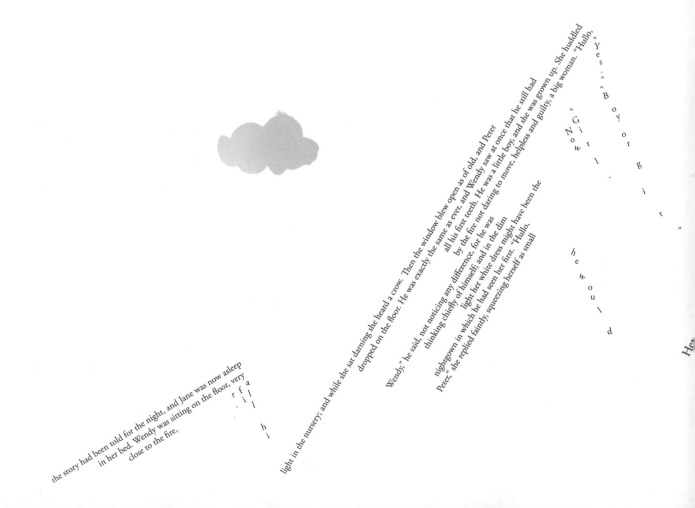

the story had been told for the night, and Jane was now asleep in her bed. Wendy was sitting on the floor, very close to the fire,

r f a
i l l
h i

light in the nursery; and while she sat darning she heard a crow. Then the window blew open as of old, and Peter dropped on the floor. He was exactly the same as ever, and Wendy saw at once that he still had all his first teeth. He was a little boy, and she was grown up. She huddled by the fire not daring to move, helpless and guilty, a big woman. "Hullo, Wendy," he said, nor noticing any difference, for he was thinking chiefly of himself; and in the dim light her white dress might have been the nightgown in which he had seen her first. "Hullo, Peter," she replied faintly, squeezing herself as small

"Hullo,
"Yes.." "Boy or girl
Now
Girl

he would

He

Peter Pan and Wendy

g would scarcely carry her now. Peter gave his nose a loving bite. She whispered in his ear "You silly ass," and then, tottering to her chamber, lay down on the bed. His head almost filled the fourth wall of her little room as he knelt near her in distress. Every moment her light was growing fainter; and he knew that if it went out she would be no more. She liked his tears so much that she thought she could get well again if children believed in fairies. Peter flung out his arms. There were no children there, and it was night-time; but he addressed all who might be dreaming of the Neverland, and who were therefore nearer to him than you think: boys and girls in their nighties, and naked papooses in their baskets hung from trees. "Do you believe?" he cried. Tink sat up in bed almost briskly to listen to her fate. She fancied she heard answers in the affirmative, and then again she wasn't sure. "What do you think?" she asked Peter. "If you believe," he shouted to them, "clap your hands; don't let Tink die." Many clapped. Some didn't. A few beasts hissed. The clapping stopped suddenly; as if countless mothers had rushed to their nurseries to see what on earth was happening; but already Tink was saved. First her voice grew strong, then she popped out of bed, then she was flashing through the room more merry and impudent than ever. She never thought of thanking those who believed, but she would have liked to get at the ones who had hissed. "And now to rescue Wendy!"

The moon was riding in a cloudy heaven when Peter rose from his perilous tree, wearing his weapons and little else, to set out upon his perilous journey. It was not such a night as he would have chosen. He had hoped to fly

The moon was riding in a cloudy heaven when Peter rose from his perilous tree, with weapons and little else, to set out upon his perilous journey. It was not such a night as he would have chosen. He had hoped to fly, and she put out her light, and that she said. Then he made it out. She was saying that she put out her light, and she ran out of the room to try to think. Peter continued to cry, and soon his sobs woke Jane. She sat up in bed, and was interested at once. "Boy," she said, "why are you crying?" Peter rose and bowed to her, and she bowed to him from the bed. "Hullo," he said. "Hullo," said Jane. "My name is Peter Pan," he told her. "Yes, I know," she said. "I come back for my mother," he explained. "Yes, I know," Jane said. "I have been waiting." "to take her to the Neverland," he told her. Peter sitting on the bed been waiting.

DISCOVER TREASURE in the DARKNESS.

with soiled blue coat, his hands ragged and scarred, bla...

I remember him as if it were yesterday, as he came plodding to the inn door, his sea-chest follo...

—a tall, strong, heavy, nut-brown man, his tarry pigtail falling over the shoulde...

and the sabre cut across one cheek...

a dirty, livid white...

It was some time before
seemed to gather our senses,

Kidnapped

I WILL BEGIN the story of
my adventures with a cer-tain
morning early in the month of June,
the year of grace 1751, when I took the key for the last time out
of the door of my father's house. The sun began to shine upon the
summit of the hills as I went down the road;
and by the time I had come as far as the manse, the blackbirds were whistling in the
garden lilacs, and the mist that hung around the valley in the time of the
and die away. Mr. Campbell, the minister of Essendean, was wait-
ing for me by the garden gate, good man! He asked me if I had breakfasted; and hearing
that I lacked for nothing,

"Well, Davie, lad," said he, "I will go with you as far as the road, to set you on the way."
And we began to walk forward in silence.

WE can lose ourselves in FORESTS of FAIRY tales

and ESCAPE MONSTERS in HAUNTED CASTLES.

she had magnificent long hair, fine as spun gold, and when she heard the voice of the prince, she unfastened her braided tresses, wound them round one of the hooks of the window above, and then the hair fell down

we will sleep

Hush-a-bye baby on the tree top, when the wind blows the cradle will rock, when the bough breaks the cradle will fall, down will fall baby, cradle and all. when the wind blows, the

Sleep serenely lovely baby, gently slumber me wherefore art smiling smiling sweet'... in though sleep? smile they see?

Lullaby and good night, with roses bedight, With lilies o'er spread is baby's wee bed. Lay thee down now and rest, may thy slumber be blessed. Lullaby and good night, with lilies o'er spread is baby's wee bed. Lay thee down now and rest, may thy slumber be blessed. Lullaby and good night, with lilies o'er spread is baby's wee bed. Lay thee down now and rest, may thy slumber be blessed. Lullaby and good night,

in clouds
of
song

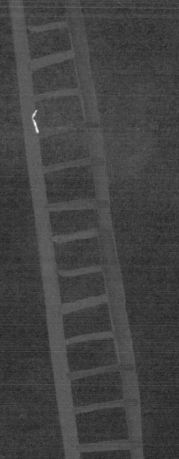

different directions, having an opportunity

could thus take observations in four of gazing at the firmament through the

Earth and the Moon through the lower and the upper lights of the Projectile.

ious to operating on the bottom light. **Around the Moon** But Barbican was the first to get th

houting: "No, my friends!" he exclaimed, in tones of decided emoti

Earth; nor are we lying in the bottom

and SHOUT as
LOUD as
we like
in SPACE.

For THIS is OUR WORLD

OUR HOUSE is a Home of

INVENTION

I am a child of books. I come from a world of stories

our world we've made from stories our house is a

where ANYONE at ALL can come

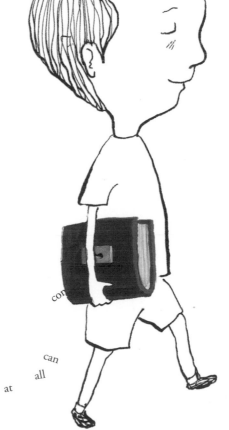

home   of   invention   where   anyone   at   all
                                                                           can
                                                                      com

For IMAGINATION is FREE

...Golden Goose *as told by Jacob Grimm and Wilhelm Grimm*, **Tom Thumb** *as told by Richard Johnson*, **The Golden Bird** *as told by Jacob Grimm and W...*

Bram Stoker ✿ THE ROPE ✿ **Rapunzel** *as told by Jacob Grimm and Wilhelm Grimm* ✿ THE CLOUDS ✿ **Suo Gân** *as adapted by Robert Bryan*, **Twinkle, Twinkle, Little Star** *by Jane Taylor*, **Hush-a-Bye Baby** *as adapted by Jo*

Alcott, **The Three Musketeers** *by Alexandre Dumas*, **The Tale of Peter Rabbit** *by Beatrix Potter*, **Alice's Adventures in Wonderland** *by Lewis Carroll*, **Great Expectations** *by Charles Dickens*, **Adventures of Huckleberry Finn** *by*

lory and Sir James Knowles and **Rip Van Winkle** *by Washington Irving* ✿ THE SEA ✿ **The Voyages of Doctor Dolittle** *by Hugh Lofting*, **The Swiss Family Robinson** *by Johann David Wyss*, **Robinson Crusoe** *by Daniel Defoe*, T

Crusoe by Daniel Defoe, **The Swiss Family Robinson** *by Johann David Wyss*, **The Adventures of Pinocchio** *by Carlo Collodi and* **Twenty Thousand Leagues Under the Sea** *by Jules Verne* ✿ THE HOLE ✿ **Alice's Adventures in**

m and Wilhelm Grimm, **Hansel & Gretel** *as told by Jacob Grimm and Wilhelm Grimm*, **The Golden Goose** *as told by Jacob Grimm and Wilhelm Grimm*, **Tom Thumb** *as told by Richard Johnson*, **The Golden Bird** *as told by Jacob G*

of Sleepy Hollow by Washington Irving, **Frankenstein** *by Mary Shelley and* **Dracula** *by Bram Stoker* ✿ THE ROPE ✿ **Rapunzel** *as told by Jacob Grimm and Wilhelm Grimm* ✿ THE CLOUDS ✿ **Suo Gân** *as adapted by Robert*

Baum, **The Wind in the Willows** *by Kenneth Grahame*, **Little Women** *by Louisa May Alcott*, **The Three Musketeers** *by Alexandre Dumas*, **The Tale of Peter Rabbit** *by Beatrix Potter*, **Alice's Adventures in Wonderland** *by Lewis*

uty by Anna Sewell, **The Legends of King Arthur and His Knights** *by Sir Thomas Malory and Sir James Knowles and* **Rip Van Winkle** *by Washington Irving* ✿ THE SEA ✿ **The Voyages of Doctor Dolittle** *by Hugh Lofting*, **The**

Sea by Jules Verne ✿ THE WAVE ✿ **Gulliver's Travels** *by Jonathan Swift*, **Robinson Crusoe** *by Daniel Defoe*, **The Swiss Family Robinson** *by Johann David Wyss*, **The Adventures of Pinocchio** *by Carlo Collodi and* **Twenty Thou**

d by Robert Louis Stevenson ✿ THE FOREST ✿ **Little Red Cap** *as told by Jacob Grimm and Wilhelm Grimm*, **Hansel & Gretel** *as told by Jacob Grimm and Wilhelm Grimm*, **The Golden Goose** *as told by Jacob Grimm and Wilhelm*

zel as told by Jacob Grimm and Wilhelm Grimm ✿ THE MONSTER ✿ **The Legend of Sleepy Hollow** *by Washington Irving*, **Frankenstein** *by Mary Shelley and* **Dracula** *by Bram Stoker* ✿ THE ROPE ✿ **Rapunzel** *as told by Jaco*

e Moon by Jules Verne ✿ THE WORLD ✿ **The Wonderful Wizard of Oz** *by L. Frank Baum*, **The Wind in the Willows** *by Kenneth Grahame*, **Little Women** *by Louisa May Alcott*, **The Three Musketeers** *by Alexandre Dumas*, Th

e Secret Garden by Frances Hodgson Burnett, **Heidi** *by Johanna Spyri*, **Black Beauty** *by Anna Sewell*, **The Legends of King Arthur and His Knights** *by Sir Thomas Malory and Sir James Knowles and* **Rip Van Winkle** *by Washing*

Gulliver's Travels by Jonathan Swift and **Twenty Thousand Leagues Under the Sea** *by Jules Verne* ✿ THE WAVE ✿ **Gulliver's Travels** *by Jonathan Swift*, **Robinson Crusoe** *by Daniel Defoe*, **The Swiss Family Robinson** *by Johan*

✿ THE CAVE ✿ **Treasure Island** *by Robert Louis Stevenson and* **Kidnapped** *by Robert Louis Stevenson* ✿ THE FOREST ✿ **Little Red Cap** *as told by Jacob Grimm and Wilhelm Grimm*, **Hansel & Gretel** *as told by Jacob Grimm*

rimm, **Beauty and the Beast** *by Jeanne-Marie Leprince de Beaumont and* **Rapunzel** *as told by Jacob Grimm and Wilhelm Grimm* ✿ THE MONSTER ✿ **The Legend of Sleepy Hollow** *by Washington Irving*, **Frankenstein** *by Mary*

ery and **Brahms' Lullaby** *by Johannes Brahms* ✿ THE MOON ✿ **Around the Moon** *by Jules Verne* ✿ THE WORLD ✿ **The Wonderful Wizard of Oz** *by L. Frank Baum*, **The Wind in the Willows** *by Kenneth Grahame*, **Little W**

n, **A Christmas Carol** *by Charles Dickens*, **Moby Dick** *by Herman Melville*, **The Secret Garden** *by Frances Hodgson Burnett*, **Heidi** *by Johanna Spyri*, **Black Beauty** *by Anna Sewell*, **The Legends of King Arthur and His Knights***

Monte Cristo by Alexandre Dumas, **Kidnapped** *by Robert Louis Stevenson*, **Gulliver's Travels** *by Jonathan Swift and* **Twenty Thousand Leagues Under the Sea** *by Jules Verne* ✿ THE WAVE ✿ **Gulliver's Travels** *by Jonathan Swift*,

nd by Lewis Carroll ✿ THE MOUNTAINS ✿ **Peter Pan and Wendy** *by J.M. Barrie* ✿ THE CAVE ✿ **Treasure Island** *by Robert Louis Stevenson and* **Kidnapped** *by Robert Louis Stevenson* ✿ THE FOREST ✿ **Little Red Cap** *as*

d Wilhelm Grimm, **Snow White and Rose Red** *as told by Jacob Grimm and Wilhelm Grimm*, **Beauty and the Beast** *by Jeanne-Marie Leprince de Beaumont and* **Rapunzel** *as told by Jacob Grimm and Wilhelm Grimm* ✿ THE MONS*

nkle, Twinkle, Little Star by Jane Taylor, **Hush-a-Bye Baby** *as adapted by John Newbery and* **Brahms' Lullaby** *by Johannes Brahms* ✿ THE MOON ✿ **Around the Moon** *by Jules Verne* ✿ THE WORLD ✿ **The Wonderful Wiza**

eat Expectations by Charles Dickens, **Adventures of Huckleberry Finn** *by Mark Twain*, **A Christmas Carol** *by Charles Dickens*, **Moby Dick** *by Herman Melville*, **The Secret Garden** *by Frances Hodgson Burnett*, **Heidi** *by Johanna*

ily Robinson by Johann David Wyss, **Robinson Crusoe** *by Daniel Defoe*, **The Count of Monte Cristo** *by Alexandre Dumas*, **Kidnapped** *by Robert Louis Stevenson*, **Gulliver's Travels** *by Jonathan Swift and* **Twenty Thousand Leag**

nder the Sea by Jules Verne ✿ THE HOLE ✿ **Alice's Adventures in Wonderland** *by Lewis Carroll* ✿ THE MOUNTAINS ✿ **Peter Pan and Wendy** *by J.M. Barrie* ✿ THE CAVE ✿ **Treasure Island** *by Robert Louis Stevenson and*

mb as told by Richard Johnson, **The Golden Bird** *as told by Jacob Grimm and Wilhelm Grimm*, **Snow White and Rose Red** *as told by Jacob Grimm and Wilhelm Grimm*, **Beauty and the Beast** *by Jeanne-Marie Leprince de Beaumont*

m Grimm ✿ THE CLOUDS ✿ **Suo Gân** *as adapted by Robert Bryan*, **Twinkle, Twinkle, Little Star** *by Jane Taylor*, **Hush-a-Bye Baby** *as adapted by John Newbery and* **Brahms' Lullaby** *by Johannes Brahms* ✿ THE MOON ✿ **Ar**

bit by Beatrix Potter, **Alice's Adventures in Wonderland** *by Lewis Carroll*, **Great Expectations** *by Charles Dickens*, **Adventures of Huckleberry Finn** *by Mark Twain*, **A Christmas Carol** *by Charles Dickens*, **Moby Dick** *by Herman*

CA ✿ **The Voyages of Doctor Dolittle** *by Hugh Lofting*, **The Swiss Family Robinson** *by Johann David Wyss*, **Robinson Crusoe** *by Daniel Defoe*, **The Count of Monte Cristo** *by Alexandre Dumas*, **Kidnapped** *by Robert Louis Stev*

tures of Pinocchio by Carlo Collodi and **Twenty Thousand Leagues Under the Sea** *by Jules Verne* ✿ THE HOLE ✿ **Alice's Adventures in Wonderland** *by Lewis Carroll* ✿ THE MOUNTAINS ✿ **Peter Pan and Wendy** *by J.M*

he Golden Goose as told by Jacob Grimm and Wilhelm Grimm, **Tom Thumb** *as told by Richard Johnson*, **The Golden Bird** *as told by Jacob Grimm and Wilhelm Grimm*, **Snow White and Rose Red** *as told by Jacob Grimm and Wilh*

✿ Bram Stoker ✿ THE ROPE ✿ **Rapunzel** *as told by Jacob Grimm and Wilhelm Grimm* ✿ THE CLOUDS ✿ **Suo Gân** *as adapted by Robert Bryan*, **Twinkle, Twinkle, Little Star** *by Jane Taylor*, **Hush-a-Bye Baby** *as adapted by Jo*

v Alcott, **The Three Musketeers** *by Alexandre Dumas*, **The Tale of Peter Rabbit** *by Beatrix Potter*, **Alice's Adventures in Wonderland** *by Lewis Carroll*, **Great Expectations** *by Charles Dickens*, **Adventures of Huckleberry Finn** *by*

alory and Sir James Knowles and **Rip Van Winkle** *by Washington Irving* ✿ THE SEA ✿ **The Voyages of Doctor Dolittle** *by Hugh Lofting*, **The Swiss Family Robinson** *by Johann David Wyss*, **Robinson Crusoe** *by Daniel Defoe*, T

Crusoe by Daniel Defoe, **The Swiss Family Robinson** *by Johann David Wyss*, **The Adventures of Pinocchio** *by Carlo Collodi and* **Twenty Thousand Leagues Under the Sea** *by Jules Verne* ✿ THE HOLE ✿ **Alice's Adventures in**

m and Wilhelm Grimm, **Hansel & Gretel** *as told by Jacob Grimm and Wilhelm Grimm*, **The Golden Goose** *as told by Jacob Grimm and Wilhelm Grimm*, **Tom Thumb** *as told by Richard Johnson*, **The Golden Bird** *as told by Jacob G*

d of Sleepy Hollow by Washington Irving, **Frankenstein** *by Mary Shelley and* **Dracula** *by Bram Stoker* ✿ THE ROPE ✿ **Rapunzel** *as told by Jacob Grimm and Wilhelm Grimm* ✿ THE CLOUDS ✿ **Suo Gân** *as adapted by Robert*

e Baum, **The Wind in the Willows** *by Kenneth Grahame*, **Little Women** *by Louisa May Alcott*, **The Three Musketeers** *by Alexandre Dumas*, **The Tale of Peter Rabbit** *by Beatrix Potter*, **Alice's Adventures in Wonderland** *by Lewis*

uty by Anna Sewell, **The Legends of King Arthur and His Knights** *by Sir Thomas Malory and Sir James Knowles and* **Rip Van Winkle** *by Washington Irving* ✿ THE SEA ✿ **The Voyages of Doctor Dolittle** *by Hugh Lofting*, **The**

Sea by Jules Verne ✿ THE WAVE ✿ **Gulliver's Travels** *by Jonathan Swift*, **Robinson Crusoe** *by Daniel Defoe*, **The Swiss Family Robinson** *by Johann David Wyss*, **The Adventures of Pinocchio** *by Carlo Collodi and* **Twenty Thou**

d by Robert Louis Stevenson ✿ THE FOREST ✿ **Little Red Cap** *as told by Jacob Grimm and Wilhelm Grimm*, **Hansel & Gretel** *as told by Jacob Grimm and Wilhelm Grimm*, **The Golden Goose** *as told by Jacob Grimm and Wilhelm*

zel as told by Jacob Grimm and Wilhelm Grimm ✿ THE MONSTER ✿ **The Legend of Sleepy Hollow** *by Washington Irving*, **Frankenstein** *by Mary Shelley and* **Dracula** *by Bram Stoker* ✿ THE ROPE ✿ **Rapunzel** *as told by Jac*

e Moon by Jules Verne ✿ THE WORLD ✿ **The Wonderful Wizard of Oz** *by L. Frank Baum*, **The Wind in the Willows** *by Kenneth Grahame*, **Little Women** *by Louisa May Alcott*, **The Three Musketeers** *by Alexandre Dumas*, Th

he Secret Garden by Frances Hodgson Burnett, **Heidi** *by Johanna Spyri*, **Black Beauty** *by Anna Sewell*, **The Legends of King Arthur and His Knights** *by Sir Thomas Malory and Sir James Knowles and* **Rip Van Winkle** *by Washing*

Gulliver's Travels by Jonathan Swift and **Twenty Thousand Leagues Under the Sea** *by Jules Verne* ✿ THE WAVE ✿ **Gulliver's Travels** *by Jonathan Swift*, **Robinson Crusoe** *by Daniel Defoe*, **The Swiss Family Robinson** *by Johan*

✿ THE CAVE ✿ **Treasure Island** *by Robert Louis Stevenson and* **Kidnapped** *by Robert Louis Stevenson* ✿ THE FOREST ✿ **Little Red Cap** *as told by Jacob Grimm and Wilhelm Grimm*, **Hansel & Gretel** *as told by Jacob Grimm*

rimm, **Beauty and the Beast** *by Jeanne-Marie Leprince de Beaumont and* **Rapunzel** *as told by Jacob Grimm and Wilhelm Grimm* ✿ THE MONSTER ✿ **The Legend of Sleepy Hollow** *by Washington Irving*, **Frankenstein** *by Mary*

ery and **Brahms' Lullaby** *by Johannes Brahms* ✿ THE MOON ✿ **Around the Moon** *by Jules Verne* ✿ THE WORLD ✿ **The Wonderful Wizard of Oz** *by L. Frank Baum*, **The Wind in the Willows** *by Kenneth Grahame*, **Little V**

n, **A Christmas Carol** *by Charles Dickens*, **Moby Dick** *by Herman Melville*, **The Secret Garden** *by Frances Hodgson Burnett*, **Heidi** *by Johanna Spyri*, **Black Beauty** *by Anna Sewell*, **The Legends of King Arthur and His Knights***

Monte Cristo by Alexandre Dumas, **Kidnapped** *by Robert Louis Stevenson*, **Gulliver's Travels** *by Jonathan Swift and* **Twenty Thousand Leagues Under the Sea** *by Jules Verne* ✿ THE WAVE ✿ **Gulliver's Travels** *by Jonathan Swift*

nd by Lewis Carroll ✿ THE MOUNTAINS ✿ **Peter Pan and Wendy** *by J.M. Barrie* ✿ THE CAVE ✿ **Treasure Island** *by Robert Louis Stevenson and* **Kidnapped** *by Robert Louis Stevenson* ✿ THE FOREST ✿ **Little Red Cap** *as*

d Wilhelm Grimm, **Snow White and Rose Red** *as told by Jacob Grimm and Wilhelm Grimm*, **Beauty and the Beast** *by Jeanne-Marie Leprince de Beaumont and* **Rapunzel** *as told by Jacob Grimm and Wilhelm Grimm* ✿ THE MON*

nkle, Twinkle, Little Star by Jane Taylor, **Hush-a-Bye Baby** *as adapted by John Newbery and* **Brahms' Lullaby** *by Johannes Brahms* ✿ THE MOON ✿ **Around the Moon** *by Jules Verne* ✿ THE WORLD ✿ **The Wonderful Wiza**

eat Expectations by Charles Dickens, **Adventures of Huckleberry Finn** *by Mark Twain*, **A Christmas Carol** *by Charles Dickens*, **Moby Dick** *by Herman Melville*, **The Secret Garden** *by Frances Hodgson Burnett*, **Heidi** *by Johanna*

ily Robinson by Johann David Wyss, **Robinson Crusoe** *by Daniel Defoe*, **The Count of Monte Cristo** *by Alexandre Dumas*, **Kidnapped** *by Robert Louis Stevenson*, **Gulliver's Travels** *by Jonathan Swift and* **Twenty Thousand Leag**

nder the Sea by Jules Verne ✿ THE HOLE ✿ **Alice's Adventures in Wonderland** *by Lewis Carroll* ✿ THE MOUNTAINS ✿ **Peter Pan and Wendy** *by J.M. Barrie* ✿ THE CAVE ✿ **Treasure Island** *by Robert Louis Stevenson an*

mb as told by Richard Johnson, **The Golden Bird** *as told by Jacob Grimm and Wilhelm Grimm*, **Snow White and Rose Red** *as told by Jacob Grimm and Wilhelm Grimm*, **Beauty and the Beast** *by Jeanne-Marie Leprince de Beaumont*

m Grimm ✿ THE CLOUDS ✿ **Suo Gân** *as adapted by Robert Bryan*, **Twinkle, Twinkle, Little Star** *by Jane Taylor*, **Hush-a-Bye Baby** *as adapted by John Newbery and* **Brahms' Lullaby** *by Johannes Brahms* ✿ THE MOON ✿ **Ar**

bit by Beatrix Potter, **Alice's Adventures in Wonderland** *by Lewis Carroll*, **Great Expectations** *by Charles Dickens*, **Adventures of Huckleberry Finn** *by Mark Twain*, **A Christmas Carol** *by Charles Dickens*, **Moby Dick** *by Herma*

CA ✿ **The Voyages of Doctor Dolittle** *by Hugh Lofting*, **The Swiss Family Robinson** *by Johann David Wyss*, **Robinson Crusoe** *by Daniel Defoe*, **The Count of Monte Cristo** *by Alexandre Dumas*, **Kidnapped** *by Robert Louis*

tures of Pinocchio by Carlo Collodi and **Twenty Thousand Leagues Under the Sea** *by Jules Verne* ✿ THE HOLE ✿ **Alice's Adventures in Wonderland** *by Lewis Carroll* ✿ THE MOUNTAINS ✿ **Peter Pan and Wendy** *by J.M*